W9-AEX-982

COULD ANYTHING BE WORSE?

Could Anything Be Worse?

A Yiddish tale retold and illustrated by

MARILYN HIRSH

Holiday House · New York

To Jim and Kadamba

Printed in the United States of America

LIBRARY OF CONGRESS CATALOGING IN PUBLICATION DATA

Hirsh, Marilyn.
Could anything be worse?

SUMMARY: Convinced nothing could be worse than the noise and confusion of his home, a man consults his rabbi who has some very wise advice.
[1. Folklore, Jewish] I. Title.
PZ8.1.H66Co 398.2 73-17364
ISBN 0-8234-0239-8

Once there lived a man who did nothing but complain about his family.

"The things that go on in my house you wouldn't believe," he told his friend. "I have no peace. What can I do?"

"Go to the Rabbi," said his friend. "He is very wise, and about family troubles he knows plenty."

So the man went home to think about his friend's advice.

"Could things be worse?" he asked himself. "No, they couldn't," he answered himself. "I'll go to the Rabbi," he said aloud.

After waiting in line he spoke to the great man.

"My daughter won't lift a finger around the house," he complained. "My wife scolds and whines. The baby screams all day and all night. The twins fight like cats and dogs, and the cat and dog fight also. Who *needs* it?"

The Rabbi nodded his head wisely. "Do you have any chickens?" he asked.

"Yes," said the man.

"Bring them into the house," ordered the Rabbi, "and ask me no questions."

The man's wife was amazed to see her husband shoo the chickens into the house.

"The Rabbi has spoken," he said.

After a miserable day and night, the man returned to the Rabbi to complain.

"On top of everything else I can't turn around without stepping on a chicken. Rabbi, what am I to do now?"

"Do you have a cow?" asked the Rabbi.

"Yes," said the man.

"Bring her into the house."

"The Rabbi has spoken," said the man to his wife as he led in the cow.

The poor man hurried back to the Rabbi full of questions, but he was afraid to ask them, so he only said, "Rabbi, help me! Now it's moo, moo, moo day and night, and the smell! I need it like a hole in the head."

"Does your wife have any poor relations?" asked the Rabbi.

"A terrible fat brother who eats without stopping and his nagging wife."

"Invite them to your home," said the Rabbi.

"I must start cooking," said his wife when she saw her brother. "Husband, such joy you've brought me!"

"What else could I do?" the man muttered to himself sadly. "The Rabbi has spoken."

Once again the man went back to the Rabbi.

"My sister-in-law complains all day. My wife is an angel next to her. My brother-in-law has eaten twelve chickens already, and my wife feeds him morning, noon, and night."

"Have your poor relations anywhere to go?"

"We have a rich cousin in the city," said the man.

"Please ask them to go there," said the Rabbi.

"The Rabbi has spoken!" cried the man in a loud, booming voice as he helped the relatives leave.

The man returned to thank the Rabbi.

"It's much better now without the relatives," the man told the Rabbi. "Of course, there's still the smell . . ."

"Does the cow have a nice stall in the barn?" asked the Rabbi.

"Yes, Rabbi, she does, and I'll put down a fresh bed of straw," said the man quickly.

"Invite the cow to return to the barn," said the Rabbi.

The cow didn't seem to understand that the Rabbi had spoken. She kept coming back to the house. But finally she was encouraged to stay in the barn.

When next the man appeared before the Rabbi, he almost looked happy.

"It smells much better at my house now," he said. "Of course, we still can't help stepping on a chicken now and then..."

Send the chickens to their coop," said the Rabbi. "They will be happier there."

"And we will be much happier without them," said the man.

"And wiser, too," said the Rabbi with a gentle smile.

"The Rabbi has spoken!" the whole family called to one another as they shooed the chickens out.

Then they threw open the windows and let the fresh air in as they cleaned and polished their home.

That evening, for the first time, the family sat down to dinner in peace. As the sun set, the man watched his wife bless the Sabbath candles.

"*Shalom*," he said to his happy family. "Our home is a paradise now."